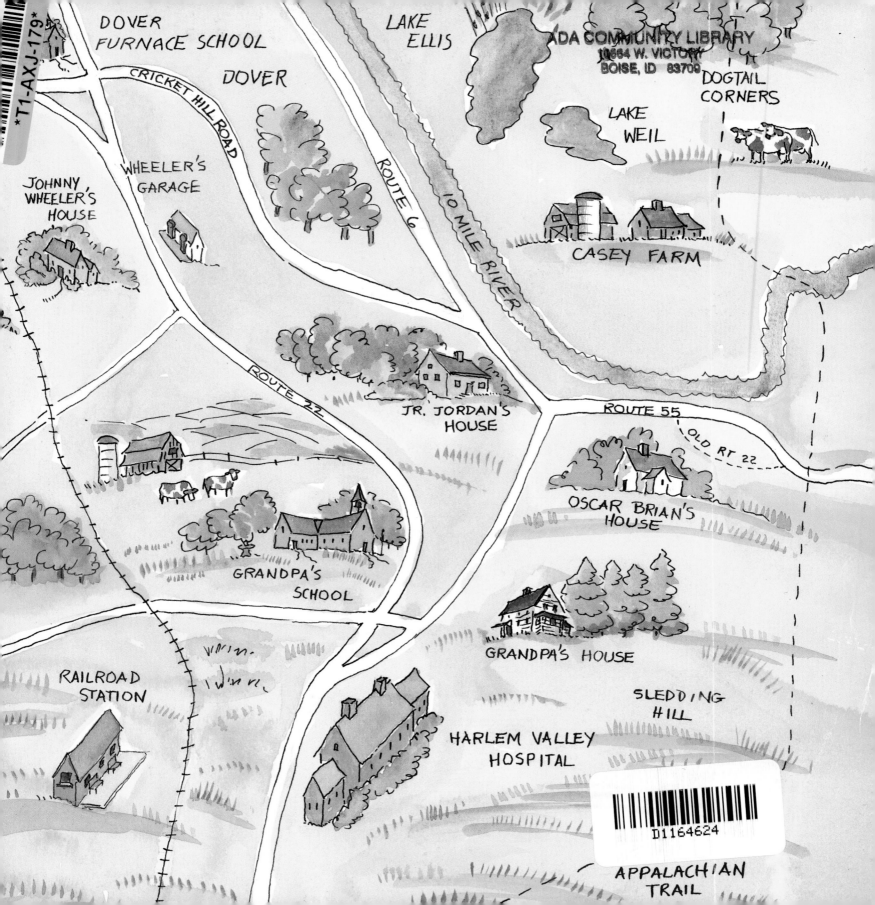

DOVER
FURNACE SCHOOL

DOVER

LAKE
ELLIS

DOGTAIL
CORNERS

LAKE
WEIL

CRICKET HILL ROAD

WHEELER'S
GARAGE

JOHNNY
WHEELER'S
HOUSE

ROUTE 6

10 MILE RIVER

CASEY FARM

ROUTE 22

JR. JORDAN'S
HOUSE

ROUTE 55

OLD RT 22

OSCAR BRIAN'S
HOUSE

GRANDPA'S
SCHOOL

GRANDPA'S HOUSE

SLEDDING
HILL

RAILROAD
STATION

HARLEM VALLEY
HOSPITAL

APPALACHIAN
TRAIL

To Benjamin and his grandpa

Copyright © 2004 by Lynne Barasch
All rights reserved
Distributed in Canada by Douglas & McIntyre Ltd.
Color separations by Chroma Graphics PTE Ltd.
Printed and bound in the United States of America by Berryville Graphics
Designed by Jennifer Crilly
First edition, 2004
1 3 5 7 9 10 8 6 4 2

www.fsgkidsbooks.com

Library of Congress Cataloging-in-Publication Data
Barasch, Lynne.
    A country schoolhouse / Lynne Barasch.— 1st ed.
       p.   cm.
    Summary: A grandfather relates to his grandson tales of the small country
school he attended in the 1940s.
    ISBN 0-374-31577-9
    [1. Schools—History—Fiction.   2. Grandfathers—Fiction.]   I. Title.

PZ7.B22965 Co 2004
[E]—dc21

                                                                        2002040759

A Country Schoolhouse

Lynne Barasch

FRANCES FOSTER BOOKS · Farrar, Straus and Giroux · New York

MY GRANDPA, the professor, walks me to school every day. He must be the smartest man in the world. I can ask him any question and he always knows the answer. Grandpa says it's thanks to the country school he went to as a boy. I never get tired of hearing him tell his story.

In 1940, when I was a little boy, I went to a small country school. There were only three rooms.

First and second grades were in one room; third, fourth, and fifth in another; and sixth, seventh, and eighth in the last.

Most of the kids in school, no matter how young, had to work a job. Their families needed them. Joseph Casey and his sister, Amelia, milked nine cows every morning before school and again in the afternoon when they got home. Joseph's arms were so strong from this, they looked like Popeye's arms. Amelia was slight, in spite of the work.

Johnny Wheeler pumped gas in his father's station every afternoon.

My dad was a doctor in the local hospital, a place with no work for a little boy. Still, I helped my family by planting, weeding, and harvesting the vegetable garden. In winter, I helped in the kitchen, peeling and chopping all the vegetables.

On my first day of school, I was given a seat in the front row, next to Billy Hample, who became my best friend. I had a new bookbag, three yellow pencils, a pink eraser, and a black-and-white notebook with lines. I liked my desk. It had a built-in inkwell. Later that year, we would learn to dip metal nib pens in the ink to write our letters. Our teacher was Miss Southworth. When she got married, she became Mrs. Rundle. We called her Miss Southworth Rundle and sometimes Miss Rundle Southworth.

We had spelling bees, geography bees, history bees, even multiplication-table bees. These were tournaments that lasted the whole year. Everyone lined up in order of age, youngest first. The line went all the way around the room. You had to answer a given question. As long as you answered correctly, you kept your place in line. But if you missed and the kid behind you got it right, he moved ahead of you.

No one wanted to be passed in the line. Unless he was careful, the passer could be tripped, accidentally on purpose. Each new day, the line started where it had ended the day before. At the end of the year, whoever was first in line was the winner. The prize was three dollars, a lot of money in those days. Of course, by that time we all knew the right answers. We had heard them hundreds of times.

"Were you the winner, Grandpa?" I asked.

"I was," Grandpa answered.

"Every year? In all the bees?" I wanted to know.

"Yes, every year," Grandpa said, "that is . . . until . . . well, but that comes later in the story."
Grandpa went on.

In the middle of the morning, we had recess in the open field next to the school. An old maple tree encircled by a bench was home base for all our games of ring-a-levio. The object of the game was to run back and forth from the fence, at one end of the field, to the bench at the other end, without being tagged.

When winter came, we had great snowball fights in the snow fort we built.

One winter, the snow was so deep, workers had to dig a tunnel for people to walk under to cross the road. Cars drove right underneath it, too!

By lunchtime, we were really hungry. We each brought our own food in a lunchbox. The kids who sat near Oscar Brian were lucky. His mother packed the best peanut-butter-and-jelly sandwiches—enough for five of us!

The schoolroom was heated by a wood-burning potbellied stove. Many a cold day we never took our coats off—or even our hats!

We had no bathroom in the school. Instead, there was a little wooden outhouse high up on the hill behind the school. In winter, we boys often didn't go all the way up there. Miss Rundle Southworth always complained, "Now, boys, don't let me see those yellow holes in the snow!" But still, we did it. The girls weren't so lucky. They had to climb all the way up to the outhouse.

One year, when we had started third grade, we found a surprise waiting for us. A shiny new tile bathroom stood inside the school! The kids stood gaping in amazement. Many of them had never seen a toilet before. They lived in farmhouses without indoor plumbing. Our teacher, Miss Berry, patiently showed us how to flush the toilet and how the seat went up and down. Even the roll of toilet paper had to be explained.

In our simple little school, every one of us learned how to locate on the map any country or city in the world. Any ocean, lake, or river. Any mountain range or any desert.

We learned the names of all the U.S. government officials: the president, the vice president, cabinet members, senators, and congressmen. We recited these facts over and over so many times, they stuck. I know them to this day. And I have always kept track of who's in office.

Since there were two or three grades in every room, you couldn't help hearing what kids in the other grades were learning. And when you forgot something, you could pick up some of last year's work to help you remember. I listened so well, I skipped fourth grade.

Luckily, even though I was small for fifth grade, I was good at baseball. That kept the farm kids off my back for skipping ahead.

Springtime brought flies. Millions of them! Over the weekend, the whole school was fumigated to kill them. On Monday, the only way we could stand the smell was to open the windows.

We had no screens, so in came more flies! Sticky flypaper hung all over the room to trap them. But it didn't help much.

One day we heard exciting news. The one-room schoolhouse in Dover Furnace, the neighboring town, shut down. The kids in that school were moving to our school! We couldn't wait to see them all! We stood outside to greet them, expecting a whole busload. Were we surprised when a pickup truck arrived and only three kids got out, two boys and a girl named Kaye Brush. No wonder they closed that school. I didn't expect that my place as number one in the spelling and history bees would be in danger.

When we lined up, I was first, as usual. The new girl was right behind me. I was asked to spell OCCASION. No problem. I knew there are two C's and one S in that word. Kaye Brush knew that, too. The teacher then went through the line and came back to me. My next word was CHRYSANTHEMUM. I spelled CHRYSANTHAMUM. Wrong! Kaye then spelled CHRYSANTHEMUM. She knew the trick! There is a THE in that word! I missed, and she moved in front of me in line—to first place! She was now number one.

"So you weren't the smartest, Grandpa?"
"So it seems," he said. He went on to finish the story . . .

When promotion day came, we had a picnic on the playing field. Everyone brought baskets of food. We all ate together and played our favorite games. Then Mr. Keyes, the principal, announced who was promoted and who was left back. Junior Jordan, fourteen years old, was finally promoted to fourth grade. For the first time, Kaye Brush won the three-dollar spelling prize and the history prize. She was better in those subjects than I was, but I won in math and geography. It was a grand day.

When I was in seventh grade, we moved to the city and I went to a big city school. It was three stories high, with long corridors and countless rooms. Not only did they have indoor bathrooms, but many of them—separate ones for boys and girls. I was overwhelmed! I never imagined such a large school.

But the biggest surprise of all was what those kids didn't know. The first day, we took a math test. Of course, in the country, I had been listening to the eighth grade all year. I finished my exam in ten minutes. The rest of the class took almost an hour. I got the highest grade, 100. The teacher held up my paper. The expression on her face said, "Look at what the hick from the country learned at his little school!" but she didn't say that. She only smiled. Little did she know that most of the country kids from our three-room school could have done just as well!

"That's a great story, Grandpa. Did you ever see Kaye Brush again?" I asked. Suddenly I realized something. "Grandpa, Kaye is Granny's name!" I said.

Grandpa laughed. "Yes, she is your granny, the girl I married years and years later. But that's another story."